American Sign Language
Alphabet Chart

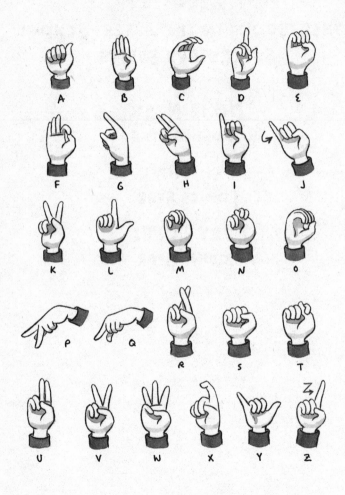

AFTER-SCHOOL SUPERSTARS

★★ BOOGIE BASS ★★
SIGN LANGUAGE STAR
WITHDRAWN

Claudia Mills

pictures by Grace Zong

MARGARET FERGUSON BOOKS
HOLIDAY HOUSE · NEW YORK

★

The publisher wishes to thank
Mary Darragh MacLean of
Sign Language Resources, Inc.
for her expert help.

Margaret Ferguson Books
Text copyright © 2021 by Claudia Mills
Pictures copyright © 2021 by Grace Zong
All Rights Reserved
HOLIDAY HOUSE is registered in the U.S. Patent and Trademark Office.
Printed and bound in June 2021 at Maple Press, York, PA, USA.
www.holidayhouse.com
First Edition
1 3 5 7 9 10 8 6 4 2

Library of Congress Cataloging-in-Publication Data

Names: Mills, Claudia, author. | Zong, Grace, illustrator.
Title: Boogie Bass, sign language star / Claudia Mills;
pictures by Grace Zong. | Description: First edition. | New York City:
Margaret Ferguson Books, | Holiday House, [2021]
Series: After-School Superstars; #4 | Audience: Ages 7–10.
Audience: Grades 2–3. | Summary: Boogie Bass feels his best friend,
Nolan, is better than he is at everything, even caring for Boogie's
little brothers, but an after-school camp reveals Boogie's talent at
communicating using American Sign Language. Includes facts about ASL.
Identifiers: LCCN 2020013531 | ISBN 9780823446292 (hardcover)
ISBN 9780823449361 (trade paperback)
Subjects: CYAC: American Sign Language—Fiction. | Family life—Fiction.
Self-confidence—Fiction. | After-school programs—Fiction.
Schools—Fiction. | Classification: LCC PZ7.M63963 Bq 2021 | DDC [Fic]—dc23
LC record available at https://lccn.loc.gov/2020013531
ISBN: 978-0-8234-4629-2 (hardcover)
ISBN: 978-0-8234-4936-1 (paperback)

★

To Kate Simpson,
my raft buddy

★

★★BOOGIE BASS★★

SIGN LANGUAGE STAR

★ one ★

Boogie Bass lifted his eyebrows, bugged out his eyes, and stretched his mouth into a grin so big it made his cheeks hurt. Maybe now his littlest brother would stop crying.

Bing didn't.

Boogie wiggled his nose. He waggled his fingers in his ears.

Bing cried even harder.

It was all Boogie's fault. He was the one who had left Bing's bedroom door open. The family dog, called Bear because he was as big as a bear, chewed anything left lying on the floor.

Shoes.

Crayons.

Homework.

The remote for the TV.

And now, Bing's little stuffed dog that he carried everywhere. Doggie-Dog no longer had a head, just a small soggy body. Boogie had banished Bear to the kitchen for this terrible crime.

As Bing clutched what was left of Doggie-Dog, Boogie picked him up and held him on his lap. He wrapped his arms around Bing's shaking shoulders.

"What do we do now?" he asked his best friend, Nolan, who had come over to spend a snowy Sunday afternoon hanging out together.

But even Nolan, the smartest kid in the entire third grade at Longwood Elementary, had nothing to offer but a sad shrug.

Boogie's dad was at work. He was a plumber. "Toilets don't just overflow on weekdays," was one of his dad's sayings. His mom was in bed with a migraine headache. Boogie knew better than to bother her unless someone was dripping blood on the carpet.

As Bing continued to sob on Boogie's lap, his other two brothers raced into the living room, the bigger one chasing the smaller one and both screaming at the top of their lungs.

"I'm going to get you!" T.J. shouted.

"Nooooo!" shrieked Gib, his shirt left behind somewhere—probably being chewed right this minute by Bear.

All four brothers had fancy names. Their mother, who was generally a very unfancy person, liked names that sounded elegant. But they had all ended up with unfancy nicknames. Nine-year-old Boogie's real name was Brewster. Six-year-old T.J.'s real name was Truman James. Four-year-old Gib's real name was Gibson. And two-year-old Bing's real name was Bingley.

"What's wrong with him this time?" T.J. asked, giving up the chase to point at Bing.

"Bear ate Doggie-Dog's head," Boogie explained.

T.J. burst out laughing. Gib, who copied everything T.J. did, laughed even harder.

"It's not funny!" Boogie told them. Except it would have been, if poor Bing wasn't crying so hard.

Boogie had to think of something to make Bing stop crying. He looked at the flakes swirling outside the window and the thick layer of snow already frosting the yard.

"Let's go sledding!"

Nolan shook his head. Boogie suddenly remembered the work it would be to dig up four snow jackets, four pairs of snow pants, four pairs of snow boots, four pairs of snow mittens, and four snow hats, plus stuff for Nolan, too.

"Let's go *indoor* sledding!" Boogie said. "The stairs can be the Olympic sledding course. No, the Olympic *luge* course. We can use the laundry basket for the luge."

Nolan shook his head again, but T.J. had already dashed into the laundry room and returned with a large plastic tub.

"There was some stuff in it, but I didn't know if it was clean or dirty, so I dumped it out on the floor," T.J. said. "Don't worry, I closed the laundry room door so Bear can't get in there to chew it. Or at least I think I did."

The next thing Boogie knew, T.J. and Gib were sitting in the laundry basket at the top of the stairs.

"Give us a push!" T.J. called to Boogie and Nolan.

"I don't think your mom is going to like

this," Nolan said to Boogie. But Boogie couldn't disappoint the others now. He set Bing down on the couch, climbed up the stairs, and gave the laundry basket a hard shove.

Down the stairs it clattered, riders screaming, Bear howling from the kitchen, where he knew he was missing out on all the fun.

"Gold medal!" T.J. shouted as they crashed into the back of the couch.

"Again!" Gib shouted. "Go fast again!"

After the second crash-landing, T.J. pumped his fist into the air. "Is there something even better than a gold medal? Like a chocolate-covered gold medal?"

"Again!" Gib continued to shout.

At least Bing had stopped crying. But Boogie saw Bing looking toward the laundry basket with longing in his eyes. Quiet little Bing hardly ever got a turn at anything.

"It's Bing's turn," Boogie announced.

"Awww!!" T.J. and Gib complained.

"It's *Bing's* turn," Boogie repeated.

Boogie carried the laundry basket back up the stairs and helped Bing, who was still clutching Doggie-Dog, climb into it.

"Ready?" he asked.

Bing pointed at Boogie, then at the basket. Bing hadn't started talking very much yet.

"You want me to get in with you?" Boogie asked. "Okay, here we go!"

Just as he shoved off, from the corner of his eye, Boogie saw Nolan frantically drawing a line across his neck with his finger, clearly the sign for *Disaster heading your way RIGHT NOW!*

Behind Nolan stood Boogie's mother.

But it was too late to stop anything.

Down went the basket, sailing past the couch this time into a narrow table, where his mother's favorite vase stood full of flowers.

Crash!

Where a vase *used* to stand, and *used* to be full of flowers.

Water splattered. Shattered pieces of glass flew everywhere. One of them hit Bing in the cheek, and he began crying again.

"Brewster Bartholomew Bass!" thundered his mother. "What on earth are you doing?"

"Um—indoor luge?"

"And whose idea was this?"

"Um—mine?"

"Oh, Boogie." Now his mother looked close to tears, too. "And they say the oldest child is supposed to be the *responsible* one. Boogie, all I wanted was one hour of peace and quiet. Not one hour of indoor luge!" She turned to Nolan. "Tell me, do *you* organize indoor Olympic winter sports at *your* house? Never mind, I know the answer to *that* one."

Nolan had already retrieved a towel, broom, and dustpan from the kitchen and was sopping up the spilled water and sweeping up the vase pieces. He spent so much time at Boogie's house he could find whatever was needed even better than the people who lived there.

Just then Boogie's mother's eyes fell upon the headless body of a certain stuffed dog that had fallen out of the laundry-basket-luge when it crashed.

"Oh, no," she said. "What happened here?"

"I left Bing's bedroom door open," Boogie muttered.

"Oh, Boogie! Nolan, in *your* house, do people forget to follow *very* simple instructions about *very* simple things like closing doors? Never mind, I know the answer to that one, too."

Boogie's mother was right.

Nolan would never think up anything as dumb as indoor luge. And Nolan would never have forgotten to keep Doggie-Dog safe from Bear.

If Nolan had been the oldest brother in Boogie's family, Bing wouldn't be in tears right now.

Boogie had always been proud to have a friend as smart as Nolan. In the after-school program they attended together, Nolan had been the best at chopping and measuring in cooking camp. In comic-book camp, Nolan had known tons of cool facts about the history of comics. In coding camp, Nolan had been the coding wizard. Boogie hadn't been very good at cooking, or drawing, *or* coding. Actually, he had been pretty terrible at all of them, but the camps had always been tons of fun.

Now they were starting a four-week sign-language camp on Monday. Boogie would bet a hundred chocolate-covered gold medals that Nolan would be really good at sign language, and a hundred times better at it than he was.

Nolan was better at *everything* than Boogie was, even better at being a brother.

"Boogie, do you ever hear *anything* I say?" his mother asked.

It was clear his mother didn't expect him to give a reply.

So Boogie helped Nolan with the sweeping as his mother carried Bing off to get a Band-Aid, leaving Doggie-Dog's headless body behind on the floor.

Maybe in sign-language camp they'd start out by learning the sign for *I'm sorry*. Right now, that would be a very useful thing for Boogie to know.

Right now, he was sorry about everything.

★ two ★

The third-grade sign-language camp was held in Boogie's old second-grade classroom. He gave a fond smile to the pictures of "community helpers" displayed on the bulletin board.

Once Colleen, the head camp lady, had checked him in, Boogie found a seat near Nolan and two other friends, chatty Nixie and quiet Vera.

"I already know the sign for *I love you*," Nixie announced.

She pointed to her chest with her index finger for *I*, folded her arms across her heart for *love*, and then pointed to the others for *you*.

Boogie didn't bother to tell Nixie that

everyone knew that one and that Nolan probably already knew a hundred signs, maybe a
thousand.

"The sign I *need* to learn is *I love dogs*,"
Nixie went on. "What do you think the sign for
dog is?"

Nixie, whose parents wouldn't let her have
a dog, loved dogs more than anyone Boogie
knew. Right now Boogie didn't even like dogs.
He still couldn't forgive Bear for what had
happened to Doggie-Dog. Last night in bed
Boogie had heard Bing whimpering in his room
for half an hour before he finally wore himself
out and fell asleep.

"How about this?" Nixie made her hands
into little begging paws and hung out her
tongue in a panting motion. "Would that be a
good sign for *dog*?"

"Sure," Nolan said. If Nolan knew the real
sign, he didn't correct Nixie. Boogie sometimes
got the feeling Nolan was almost embarrassed
at knowing more about everything than everybody else.

"Shush." Vera, who had been silently doo-
dling in her art notebook, laid down her pencil

and put her finger to her lips. "The teachers are going to start talking."

Vera was the one who cared most about hearing every word every teacher ever said and who worried most if she missed a single instruction.

The teacher standing closer to the door switched the classroom lights off and on three times. The room of campers quieted instantly.

For this camp, both teachers were women. One teacher was short and round with curly hair boinging out all over her head like the springs of an out-of-control jack-in-the-box. The other teacher had long, straight hair that matched her tall, thin body. She was the one who had flicked the light switch.

"I see that worked," she said with a grin. "If you were a class of Deaf or hard-of-hearing students, I wouldn't have been able to get your attention by calling out 'Hey!' or clapping my hands, right? You'd need a visual cue, and one that didn't depend on your looking straight at me, either. That's one of the things you're going to be learning about Deaf culture this month."

Maybe Boogie's mom should try the light-switch trick at home. T.J. and Gib were so used to her yelling they hardly heard it anymore. Or if they heard, they didn't listen.

"I am *Peg*," the tall teacher said, talking with her hands now as well as with her voice. The motions she made with her fingers must have been spelling out her name. "I am *hearing*." She moved her index finger in a small circle in front of her mouth.

Peg continued to talk. "This is *Sally*. She is *Deaf*." The shorter, curly-haired teacher placed her finger by her ear and moved it near her lips. That must be the sign for saying you weren't hearing.

Peg explained that American Sign Language, or ASL, started to develop over two hundred years ago. A man named Thomas Hopkins Gallaudet went all the way to Europe to learn the best way of teaching Deaf students. There, he met a famous Deaf teacher from France named Laurent Clerc. Together, back in the United States, they combined French Sign Language with the signs that Deaf people in America were already using among themselves.

This became ASL. In addition to the millions of Deaf people who now communicated through ASL, some parents used sign language with their hearing babies and toddlers who couldn't speak words aloud yet. It was a beautiful way for anybody to be able to communicate.

The campers were going to start by learning the ASL alphabet. Sign language had the same ABCs as spoken language, but instead of being said out loud, or written on a piece of paper, the letters were formed with your fingers. Sally and Peg explained these were called "handshapes": the shapes of your hands when they make a letter or a sign.

Sally passed out sheets of paper showing pictures of a hand in twenty-six different positions, one for each letter of the alphabet.

Boogie started to have a bad feeling. Twenty-six of anything was a lot to remember. There were only twelve times tables in math, and Boogie was already stuck on his sixes. Now he imagined himself stuck on K, or L, or M, while Nolan would know all twenty-six letters after the very first day. Probably Nolan knew all twenty-six letters already.

Just the way Nolan had already known indoor luge was a bad idea.

Just the way Nolan would have remembered to close Bing's bedroom door.

"We aren't going to learn every single letter today," Peg reassured the campers, as if she had been reading Boogie's thoughts.

Boogie was glad to hear that.

Peg continued, "It will help a lot if you take this paper home and practice the letters for ten minutes every evening."

Boogie wasn't glad to hear that.

He already had to practice his multiplication facts, and work on his inventor report for Mrs. Townsend, and walk Bear, and take turns with T.J. for setting and clearing the table. None of the other camps had *homework*.

The whole time Peg was talking, Sally had been making motions with her hands— probably signing the words for *paper* and *home* and *practice* and *ten minutes* and *every evening*.

How would anyone ever learn all those words? And how to put them together into sentences?

Sign language was going to be impossible!

The team of Peg-and-Sally told them to start with the letters for their names. Spelling out a word letter-by-letter was called "finger-spelling." For finger-spelling, and all signs made with just one hand, you used your dominant hand, the hand you used to write or eat. So as a right-handed person, Boogie would form the letters with his right hand.

Boogie had the longest name in his group, but two of the letters were the same. Luckily, *O* looked like an *O*, with fingers and thumb curled to form a circle. The letter *I* looked like an *I*, with the pinkie pointed straight up in the air. Some of the other ASL letters looked like themselves, too. For the *V* in her name, Vera held her forefinger and middle finger apart to form a *V*. The *L* in Nolan's name was forefinger and thumb held in an *L* shape.

Maybe sign language wasn't going to be impossible, after all. Though there would still be hundreds—no, thousands—of whole entire words to learn.

When it came time to go around the room finger-spelling their names, Sally, the Deaf teacher, said each letter aloud as they spelled it. How could a Deaf person talk if she couldn't hear? Peg told them that some people who were Deaf from birth learned how to make sounds by studying how hearing people held their lips and tongues. Sally's voice sounded different from Peg's voice—the sounds were harder to tell apart—but most of the time Boogie could understand what she was saying.

"B–O–O–G," she said as Boogie awkwardly held up his fingers, one letter at a time.

"E–R!" called out a kid named James, who was always trying to be funny, often at Boogie's expense.

Some kids laughed.

Flustered now, Boogie made the sign for *E* instead of for *I*, as if he really was spelling B–O–O–G–E–R instead of B–O–O–G–I–E, and then he forget which letters he was supposed to be signing.

Quickly, Nolan held up his fingers for an *I* and *E*, so Boogie could copy them.

"I–E," Sally said, giving Boogie a reassuring smile.

"Thanks," Boogie whispered to Nolan as

Nolan perfectly spelled out N-O-L-A-N without any hesitation.

Nolan helped Nixie make the letters in her name, too. Nixie had been too busy learning the letters for D-O-G to get around to the letters for N-I-X-I-E.

Boogie was lucky to have a best friend who was smart *and* kind *and* helpful to everyone.

But was Nolan lucky to have a best friend who couldn't even remember how to spell his own name?

And who wasn't a very good big brother, either?

★ three ★

At home that evening, Boogie got ready to take Bear for a short walk around the block so the dog could do his peeing-and-pooping business. At the sight of the leash, Bear wagged his huge tail so hard it could have knocked over Gib or Bing—maybe even T.J., too. Usually Boogie played a keep-away game with the leash before snapping it onto Bear's collar, but he didn't want Bear to think he was forgiven for his crime against Doggie-Dog.

"Bad dog!" he told Bear crossly, even though he knew Bear had no idea what he was being scolded for now. Besides, it had all really been Boogie's fault, not Bear's.

Back from the walk, Boogie organized a game of build-a-tower-and-knock-it-down. It was T.J. and Gib's favorite game, though it sometimes turned into knock-it-down-and-then-throw-the-blocks-all-over-the-place, which was his mother's least favorite game. Bing liked the building part better than the wrecking part, but even Bing usually squealed with laughter when the blocks went flying. But today Bing gave a small sad smile.

Was there any way to sew a new head on Doggie-Dog's body and make him as good as new?

Boogie could already think of three problems with this plan.

1. He had no idea where to find a new Doggie-Dog head. Stuffed toys didn't come with extra heads for dog-chewing emergencies.

2. Boogie didn't know how to sew.

3. And where was Doggie-Dog's body, anyway? Had his mom already thrown it away?

Boogie tried to recall where he had last seen Doggie-Dog's body. Bear had come into the family room carrying it in his mouth, while Bing had followed behind wailing. Boogie had managed to get the body away from Bear—and it was never easy to get any chewable object away from Bear—and then he had given it back to Bing and comforted him as best he could. Then the luge accident happened, and his mother saw Doggie-Dog-without-a-head, and carried Bing off to get bandaged.

But what had happened next with the rest of Doggie-Dog?

Now he remembered: he had stuffed it under the couch cushion so Bing wouldn't see it and start crying again. Besides, a headless dog was too depressing for anybody.

Sure enough, when Boogie lifted up the cushion, there it was, along with a remote for a TV they no longer owned, an empty potato chip bag, dried-out Silly Putty, around four thousand broken crayons, and his father's lost set of car keys.

Hiding Doggie-Dog's body behind his back, Boogie slipped away upstairs. Then he tucked it into the bottom of his bureau drawer.

Now all he needed to do was find a dog head somewhere.

And learn to sew somehow.

★ ★ ★

When Tuesday's camp began, Boogie managed to finger-spell his name perfectly on the first try. But as Peg and Sally led the campers through the first few letters of the alphabet, it was clear he didn't know any of them except for the *B* and *E* from his name. But it was equally clear most of the other campers hadn't practiced, either.

Vera knew every single letter, but she frowned so hard with worry over each one that it looked as if she was signing an ABC of owies. *A* for Ankle sprain, *B* for Bonked on the head, *C* for Cut finger. . . . What would *D* be for? Maybe *D* for Disaster while luging on the stairs.

"Boogie, are you with us?" Peg interrupted his thoughts as Sally came to his desk to help form his fingers into the signs for *F* and *G*. At least Sally had been the one who helped him this time instead of Nolan.

"Help *me*!" Nixie begged Sally, even though Sally couldn't hear and wasn't looking her way. Then Nixie tugged on Sally's sleeve, and Sally turned around to face her. "I forgot *H*!" Nixie wailed.

Boogie suspected Nixie hadn't "forgotten" *H*, but had never known it in the first place. But as Sally helped Nixie make the sign for *H*, Nixie looked as pleased with herself as if she had known it all along.

After *J*, Peg declared that was enough alphabet for one day. Boogie couldn't have agreed more.

He was relieved when Sally turned on a video of a Deaf family having breakfast together and signing the words for everything they were eating.

The Deaf family in the video had a mother, father, brother, sister, and dog. They sat in their tidy kitchen at the neatly prepared table and politely asked each other to pass the milk, the juice, the eggs, the toast, the pancakes, the coffee. Even the dog politely lay on the floor patiently waiting until the boy in the video slipped him a piece of bacon.

They couldn't have been more opposite from Boogie's family.

Nobody grabbed.

Nothing spilled.

The parents didn't yell.

Well, Deaf parents would probably yell with their hands, not their voices. But these parents didn't yell at all, and Boogie's parents yelled with their hands *and* their voices.

Boogie was amazed.

Unfortunately, he was so busy being amazed by the Deaf family's peaceful breakfast that he hardly paid attention to the signs for the different kinds of food they were eating. But as Peg and Sally explained the signs afterward, he was amazed by those, too. Whoever had thought up the signs was a total sign-thinking-up genius.

The sign for *milk* was to open and close your fist like you were milking a cow—not that Boogie, or anyone else in the class probably, had ever milked a cow.

The sign for *egg* wasn't to make your fingers into a circle, as Boogie would have expected. It was to hold two fingers together on each hand, with the hands almost touching each other, and then move the hands apart in a jerky motion, like breaking eggs.

The sign for *coffee* was a twisting motion of both fists, one on top of the other, as if you were grinding coffee beans.

In the sign for "*Good morning*"—this family was so polite that they started breakfast by saying "Good morning" to one another—you showed *morning* by making your dominant arm rise up like the sun from the "horizon" of the other arm, held horizontally across your body.

How many Deaf people had it taken to think up all these signs? That would have been a huge job.

And who had thought up the English language words for *milk*, *eggs*, *coffee*, *morning*?

It was strange to think there was a word for everything that ever existed, in every language including sign language. But the signs in sign language were a lot cooler than saying plain old words.

Next Sally and Peg produced a crate full of toy food, the kind that used to be in the toy kitchen at Boogie's house until it had all gotten lost over the years. Boogie was surprised he hadn't found a toy cheeseburger or toy ice-cream cone under the couch cushion where he had hidden what was left of Doggie-Dog. The teachers spread the toy food out on a table in front of the room, like a buffet at a restaurant.

Peg told the campers to divide themselves into teams. Boogie's team was Nolan, Nixie, and Vera, of course. Each team was supposed to pretend to be having breakfast together. One person would sign "I want an egg"; the sign for *want* was to pull an imaginary object toward yourself with both hands, palms up. Then the person sitting next to you would run to get that item from the table. If it was correct, you'd sign "thank you" by touching your chin and then moving your hand away. The first team to have a full breakfast would be the winner. Boogie saw a bag of candy on the teacher's desk, so maybe the winning team would each get a piece of candy.

"Ready, set, go!" Peg called out.

Nixie brought Nolan coffee when he had asked for milk. But she raced back with the correct beverage after Nolan made the sign for *no*, which was not shaking your head, which would have made sense to Boogie, but tapping two fingers against your thumb in a sort of snapping motion.

Nolan brought Vera her orange juice. Boogie hadn't expected any mistakes from those two.

Vera brought Boogie his toast. So he must have done a good job of making two fingers on his right hand look like a fork quickly poking into each side of his left hand, as it was a piece of bread. It was so cool that someone could know exactly what you were saying without anybody speaking aloud a single word.

When it was Boogie's turn to take Nixie's order, Nixie signed that she wanted two eggs. First she held up two fingers, then she made the sign for egg. Two eggs, coming right up!

James was at the table as Boogie dashed over to it.

"What are you getting?" James asked him, even though there wasn't supposed to be any talking during the game.

Boogie knew he should have ignored

James, but instead he signed *two eggs* in the same way Nixie had.

Bad mistake.

Peg and Sally were both busy helping campers who had forgotten the signs for *orange juice* and *pancakes*.

"Catch!" James said.

Boogie tried to catch the eggs as James tossed them to him, but one struck him in the arm and the other rolled across the floor.

"Boys!" Colleen, who as head camp person was in charge of discipline, appeared out of nowhere. Her scolding voice made it sound like the egg disaster was Boogie's fault as much as James's. Then again, Boogie was the one who had dropped an egg on the floor during cooking camp. He was the one who had knocked a cup of juice all over the work table during comic book camp.

That was the trouble with being a klutz. You got blamed for things even when you weren't being klutzy. Though maybe if Boogie had been better at catching, he would have snagged both eggs and raced back to his team with them already.

Peg switched the lights off and on.

"We have a winner!" she announced.

She tossed a piece of candy to each member of the team that came in first—not James's team and certainly not Boogie's.

Every single person caught their pieces of candy with no problem at all.

★ four ★

"**G**uess who just peed in his pants?" T.J. asked at breakfast the next morning.

This was definitely not how breakfast began in the Deaf family video.

Boogie wondered what the sign for *peed in his pants* would be. He didn't suppose they'd learn something like that at sign-language camp.

His mother didn't even need to guess. "Oh, Bing," she said. "You're having a potty accident every day now." She scooped Bing up and carried him off to change him out of his damp jeans and underwear.

"Catch!" Boogie's father said as two frozen waffles popped out of the toaster.

"Me!" shouted T.J.

"Me!" shouted Gib.

Their dad sent a waffle flying through the air to each of them. T.J. caught his; Gib missed, but at least his landed on the table, not the floor.

"Dad?" Boogie asked as his father put two more waffles in the toaster. He wanted to ask his question while Bing was out of the room. "Do you know anyplace where I can buy a new head for Doggie-Dog?"

"A new *what* for *who*?" his dad asked.

His dad worked such long hours that he didn't even know the name of Bing's favorite stuffed animal. This was the first time his dad had been home for breakfast in ages.

"A new head for Bing's stuffed dog. Bear ate the old one," Boogie explained. "All that's left is the body."

"Maybe if you buy a whole new stuffed dog, this time Bear will eat the body," his dad suggested with a chuckle. "Then all that's left will be the head. So you'll have one body without a head and one head without a body. Problem solved."

This sent T.J. off into gales of giggles,

followed by more copycat giggles from Gib.

"What's so funny?" Boogie's mom asked, coming into the room with Bing, now dressed for the day in clean, dry clothes.

"I just wanted"—Boogie lowered his voice— "to find out how to get a new you-know-what for you-know-who." He gave a meaningful look in Bing's direction.

His mother sighed. "Let's not start that all over again. I've spent half of my life this past year looking for you-know-what every time he was lost, or forgotten somewhere, or left under a tree. I'm starting to think all this fuss about stuffed animals is more trouble than it's worth."

She whirled around to see two more waffles flying through the air.

"Brian!" she scolded her husband. "You're as bad as the boys!"

"Worse," Boogie's dad said with a grin.

It was clear to Boogie that if a new head was going to be found for Doggie-Dog, Boogie was going to have to find it all by himself.

At camp that afternoon, the Deaf family in the video was eating lunch, with no food objects flying through the air. Sally and Peg had brought another crate of toy food, featuring lunch items. This time they organized a scavenger hunt, where one camper, with Sally's help, would sign a particular food, and the other campers would dash around the room to find it.

Peg had to switch the lights off and on several times, as James and another boy had a tug-of-war over a plastic cheeseburger and Vera tripped when another kid mowed her down in search of a slice of plastic watermelon.

Boogie would never have guessed learning a new language could be so violent and dangerous. Practicing the ASL alphabet was boring, but definitely caused fewer scuffles and injuries.

On Thursday the Deaf family talked with their hands about getting dressed. The best part was when the boy in the video put a hat and scarf on the dog. Nixie was thrilled with the sign for *dog*: you tapped your thigh and then snapped your fingers with the same hand, as if you were calling, *Here, boy!* or *Here, girl!*

The Deaf family didn't have a cat, but Sally

taught the campers the sign for *cat*: tracing imaginary whiskers on your face. Life would be so much more interesting if everybody talked in sign language!

"Now I can tell my parents I want a dog in four different languages," Nixie said as they practiced the signs from the video afterward. "I already know how to say *dog* in French and Spanish: *chien* and *perro*. And in English, of course: *dog, dog, dog, dog, DOG!* And now: tap your thigh and snap your fingers. Tap and snap! I'm going to keep on tapping and snapping until they can't take it anymore." Nixie gave a few more taps and snaps, as if her new dog would come bounding up to her any minute.

Across the room, Boogie could see James rolling his eyes as other kids were signing, as if it was the dumbest thing in the world to touch the top of your head twice for *hat*, or tap your two fists together twice for *shoes*. James always acted like everything they learned in all the after-school camps was silly.

But Boogie thought James was the silly one for thinking that.

★ ★ ★

"Today is *feelings* day," Peg said out loud on Friday afternoon, while Sally signed the same thing. Peg told the campers sign language was especially good at showing emotion, because emotions were always communicated best through facial expression and gestures.

Sure enough, when Sally made the sign for *happy*—rubbing her hands up her chest with a circular motion while giving a huge grin—she *looked* happy. For *sad*, she ran her spread fingers down in front of her face like tears. What could look sadder than that? For *scared*, she held her fists near her chest, then opened them up suddenly and crossed her arms at the same time. The fright showed in her face as well.

"Practice feelings signs for a while in your usual groups," Peg told them.

Vera made the *happy* hand motions, with a worried face.

She made the *sad* hand motions, with a worried face.

She made the *scared* hand motions, with a worried face.

"What's the sign for *worried*?" Boogie called over to Peg.

She came to their cluster of desks and made her fingers into B-letter handshapes, moving them around as if swatting pesky flies away from her face. As she did it, she furrowed her forehead in a worried way.

"Do that one, Vera," Boogie told her with a grin.

Vera jabbed him in the shoulder. "I don't look worried *all* the time, do I?" she said, looking worried as she said it.

Nolan was the best—of course—at remembering exactly how to make each sign, but his *happy*, *sad*, and *scared* faces looked stiff and wooden, more like someone pretending to feel those things.

Nixie's problem was that she started giggling after every feelings sign. Boogie could tell she wasn't making fun of sign language, the way James sometimes seemed to be doing. She was just laughing because she felt silly making the faces.

As Boogie tried out his signs, Sally tapped

him on the shoulder after the last one. When he turned to look at her, she made the sign for *Good!* three times, moving her hand forward from her chin in a sort of bow.

Boogie didn't think his feelings signs had been *good, good, good.* Well, maybe he had done better with feelings than Vera, Nolan, and Nixie, but he was still the worst of anyone at remembering the letters of the alphabet.

Sally tapped Boogie on the shoulder again and made a sign that seemed to mean she wanted him to go to the front of the room. Peg saw her and translated.

"Campers, watch Boogie! He's doing a great job of signing feelings in a natural, believable way."

Boogie came to the front of the room. What other choice did he have? But now he felt like someone acting in a not-very-good play called *How to Show Your Feelings*. Not like a real kid feeling happy, sad, or scared. Well, sort of like a real kid feeling scared. What if the other campers laughed? What if James started laughing, and then the others laughed along with him?

But to his surprise, the other campers clapped when he finished, after adding in the sign for *worried*, as well. He could hear Nixie bragging to the kids sitting behind her. "Boogie has a *huge* dog, too, and I walked him once!"

Peg demonstrated the Deaf way of applauding, by raising your hands, spreading your fingers, and twisting them silently in the air. Then the campers twisted their raised hands for Boogie, too.

As he headed back to his seat, he passed James. "Nice job, Boogie," James mocked, making the *scared* sign in an extra-exaggerated way. James hadn't joined in the hearing *or* the Deaf clapping.

Boogie thought about walking past James as if he hadn't noticed. But he laughed and made the *happy* sign in reply, with an extra-happy grin.

He *was* happy right now, James or no James.

★ five ★

If he couldn't buy a new Doggie-Dog head, Boogie would have to buy a whole new Doggie-Dog, the way his dad had suggested. Not so Bear could chew off this Doggie-Dog's body. Boogie couldn't bring himself to treat an innocent stuffed animal in that way. Besides, Bear didn't need any encouragement for his chewing habits.

Boogie would make up some story about how a headless, dirty, worn-out dog had turned into a brand-new one, complete with unchewed head and clean, fresh fur. But first he had to get the brand-new one. How was he supposed to do that?

He couldn't ask his mom to help him. She had already said she didn't want to *start that all over again.*

He couldn't ask his dad to help him. His dad was always at work. Not that his dad had taken Doggie-Dog's tragedy very seriously, anyway.

So the only person he could ask was Nolan.

On Saturday morning he rode his bike to Nolan's house. Instead of three younger brothers, Nolan had two older sisters. To them, Nolan was the baby of the family. Boogie bet that even as a baby Nolan had been brilliant. He grinned, imagining baby Nolan sucking on his ten fingers and ten toes and then saying, in an itty-bitty voice, *Ten plus ten equals twenty*.

Nolan's house was neat and tidy, like the house of the Deaf family in the video. Boogie was sure if he lifted up the couch cushions he would find no empty potato chip bags or lost sets of car keys. But it was still cozy and homey.

The best thing in it was an orange elephant taller than Bing, made of fabric with dozens of tiny mirrors sewed into it, sparkling in the light from the living room fireplace. In Boogie's house that elephant would have been ridden to death by T.J. and Gib, and Bear would have chewed off its trunk.

"I have a problem," Boogie said, once he and Nolan were settled on the couch by the elephant with a plate of cookies baked by one of Nolan's sisters who was taking a Food Fun class at her middle school. Boogie bit into the first one. "A-plus!" he mumbled over a mouthful of chocolate chips and walnuts. Even the cookies were better at Nolan's house.

"I want to get Bing a new Doggie-Dog," Boogie told Nolan after swallowing. "But I don't know where to find one."

"Let's look online," Nolan said.

Sure enough, after a few clicks by Nolan on his laptop—Nolan had his very own computer—there on the screen was a stuffed dog that looked exactly like Doggie-Dog, complete with head.

"Kids can't buy things online," Boogie pointed out. "We don't have the right kind of cards to pay for them."

"I'll ask my mom to order one for us, and we can pay her back," Nolan said. He checked the price. "It's eighteen dollars, plus four dollars for shipping. No problem!"

No problem?

It might as well be a million dollars plus a hundred thousand dollars for shipping.

"I only have sixty-seven cents," Boogie confessed.

"Well, *I* can pay *her* back *now*, and then *you* can pay *me* back *later*."

Nolan made it sound so simple. Boogie thought about how much Bing missed Doggie-Dog. If he said, *Thanks, Nolan, that would be great*, Bing could be hugging a brand-new Doggie-Dog in a few days.

But then he imagined his mother saying to Nolan, *Do* you *spend every penny of* your *allowance on junk food and even junkier toys, or do* you *save* yours *so you* have money to buy nice things for *other* people? Never mind, I already know the answer to *that* one.

"That's okay," Boogie said. "I'll save up the money, and then you can ask your mom to buy it for me."

But with two dollars allowance a week, it would take the rest of Boogie's life, practically, for him to buy Bing a new Doggie-Dog. Nolan would know how to do the math to figure out exactly how long, but Boogie wasn't going to ask him. He couldn't ask Nolan *everything*.

He'd just have to earn extra money somehow.

But how?

He wasn't going to ask Nolan that, either.

By the middle of the second week of sign-language camp, Boogie loved every single thing about sign language except for the alphabet. Why did alphabets need twenty-six letters? It took forever for little kids to learn the plain old ABCs, even with a special catchy song made up to help them remember the letters in order. When he was little, Boogie had thought *L-M-N-O-P* was some weird letter with an extra-long name.

Now in camp they were signing the alphabet while chanting the ABC song very, very slowly, to give everyone enough time to get their hands in position for each letter. But it still wasn't slow enough for Boogie to keep up.

If Boogie had been inventing sign language, he would have written each letter in the air with his pointer finger. Well, maybe that wouldn't work, because the letters would look backward to the person reading them, like mirror writing.

If Boogie were teaching a sign-language camp, he would skip over the ABCs and go straight to the signs for actual words. But some of the word signs used the alphabet letters: for example, to sign the days of the week, you had to make *M* for *Monday*, *T* for *Tuesday*, *W* for *Wednesday*, and move each letter sign around in a small circle.

Anyway, Boogie wasn't in charge of any of this.

On Wednesday, Sally made the sign for *sad* when Boogie still got stuck on most of the letters. And the sign for *sad*—those fake tears running down Sally's cheeks—was sadder than spelling out *sad* would have been.

"Campers," Peg said to the whole roomful of kids, "believe me, it will make a *big* difference if you *practice* the alphabet at home just *ten* minutes a *day*."

But it was clear the only person who hadn't learned his ABCs yet was Boogie. Even James, who acted like he didn't care about sign language at all, had apparently managed to learn the letters just from the time spent on them in class. Boogie doubted that Nixie was practicing very hard, either. Everyone else just seemed better at memorizing alphabet letters than he was.

James caught Boogie's eye and signed the letter *L*, one of the letters Boogie did know because it looked like the *L* kids made to call each other a *loser*. He knew that was how James meant it, too.

Should Boogie just ignore James? Or maybe it would be better to act like he didn't mind the joke? So he pointed to himself with a smile of fake pride, as if he thought James was being funny, not mean. *A loser? That's me!*

But *loser* did seem like a pretty good description of someone whose fingers still couldn't remember the ABCs little Deaf kids learned when they were babies.

★ six ★

After the disastrous ABC practice that day, Peg and Sally showed a video of the Deaf family taking a walk in the park and signing the words for the things they saw on their way. For *tree,* they held their left arm flat as if it was the ground; they held their right arm with the elbow touching the back of the left hand, straight up like the trunk of a tree, and twisted their fingers like tree branches blowing in the wind. For *bicycle,* they moved their fists like feet pedaling.

Then Peg made an announcement. On Friday, they were going to have a camp field trip to an after-school program at a school across town. The students at Laurent Clerc School were all Deaf or hard-of-hearing.

"They will put on a special program for us," Peg said as Sally signed. "But there will also be a chance for you to meet the students there and chat with them, showing how much ASL you have already learned in our camp's first two weeks. So we will spend today and tomorrow learning some basic questions and answers for making conversation."

Sally showed the campers how to sign *What is your name?* and *What is your favorite food?*, plus a few other things, and then it was time for the campers to practice with one another. At least the sign for *Hi* was an easy one: moving your hand out from your forehead in a sort of salute. Maybe Boogie could just say hi over and over again to lots of different people.

"What if we mess up?" Vera asked Boogie, Nolan, and Nixie. "What if none of those kids can understand a single thing we try to say? Or what if we try to make the sign for one thing, but it's the sign for another thing, and the other thing is something really embarrassing?"

"We won't," Nixie promised her.

Nixie was always sure everything was going to be great.

"Or if we do, it'll just be funny," Nixie went on. "And they'll laugh, and we'll laugh. And maybe one of them will have a dog that just had puppies, and she'll ask if we know anyone who has a good home for a puppy, and I'll sign, *YES!* What do you think the signs would be for *My dog just had puppies*?"

"Oh, Nixie," Vera said. "We could never understand the signs for a complicated thing like that. You know we couldn't. Even Nolan couldn't."

Boogie certainly couldn't. But at least it was unlikely any of the Deaf kids would quiz him on his ABCs.

"We could practice the alphabet together," Nolan offered as he and Boogie sat side by side at the end of camp the next day waiting for their parents to come pick them up. Sally hadn't made the *sad* sign after Boogie messed up the alphabet yet again. She had given Peg a look that might as well have been the sign for *annoyed*. "I've been having trouble remembering some of the letters, too," Nolan added.

Liar! You never forget anything!

But Boogie didn't say that out loud. He knew Nolan was just trying to be a good friend.

"I'm okay," Boogie said cheerfully. "Maybe there will be a camp booby prize for worst at ABCs, and I'll get it, and it'll turn out to be something really cool. Remember that one birthday party we went to where the mom gave a prize to the kid who hadn't won any of the other prizes, and it was this really great game, and the kids who won real prizes were mad because theirs were just candy and stickers?"

"We could even practice a little bit right now," Nolan said, ignoring Boogie's reply. "How about we start with *M*?"

"How about we don't?" Boogie said, less cheerfully this time, and Nolan dropped the subject.

But that evening Boogie looked for his alphabet handout. He finally found it crumpled in the bottom of his backpack. He made himself practice for ten minutes. Then he figured he might as well practice for ten minutes more.

When Boogie got off the bus with the other campers on Friday and filed into the Deaf school, Laurent Clerc Elementary looked just like Longwood Elementary: office by the front door, student artwork hanging in the halls, gym with basketball hoops. But it didn't sound like Longwood Elementary. To Boogie's surprise it was much noisier! Footsteps pounded down the hallway; lockers slammed; he could hear kids laughing so loudly Boogie's classroom teacher would have shushed them.

A group of the Deaf students were clustered by the stage at one end of the gym talking together in sign language. Even though Boogie knew he should have expected this, he was amazed by how fast the kids—some his age, some even younger—were moving their hands. The Deaf kids in the videos could sign fast, too, of course, but this wasn't a video, it was real life.

Boogie couldn't recognize any of their signs; they all went by so quickly. But the Deaf kids seemed to understand each other perfectly. One of them must have said something funny, because the others burst out laughing.

Boogie was glad he had practiced the alphabet last night. If the Deaf kids could do such amazing things with their hands and faces, he could at least try to learn the difference between *M* and *N*.

"Wow," he heard Nixie say under her breath as she watched the Deaf students, too.

It was like the Olympics on TV, with the ice skaters leaping into the air and twirling three times before landing, only these were regular kids talking the way they did every day.

"Can you understand anything they're saying?" Vera whispered to Nolan.

Nolan shook his head.

Boogie couldn't tell if Vera was relieved or even more worried. If Nolan couldn't figure out the Deaf kids' signs, how could the rest of them have a conversation with anybody about anything?

At that moment, one of the Deaf teachers turned the gym lights off and on the way Peg and Sally did at camp, but he had to flash the lights at least ten times before the Deaf kids stopped moving their hands and looked instead at their teachers. It was clearly time for the program to begin.

The first number on the program was four kids dancing to music played super loud from large speakers on either side of the stage. They danced to the rhythm exactly as if they could hear every beat. One of the Deaf teachers, who spoke while he signed, explained that the students felt the rhythm from the vibrations of the pounding bass in the music. Also, deafness was a matter of degree; not all Deaf people were completely unable to hear any sounds at all.

Boogie had gotten his nickname because he used to boogie to music when he was Bing's age. But whenever he danced, he ended up tripping over his shoes or bumping into somebody. These kids were as quick and graceful with their feet as they were with their hands.

Then the Deaf students took turns telling a bunch of very short stories, using the letters of the alphabet. It took Boogie a few moments to catch on, because they weren't using the letters to stand for words that *started* with the letter, such as *A* for *apple* or *B* for *bear*, like in all the other ABC storybooks he had ever seen.

Instead, they used the *shapes* of the letters, in order from *A* to *Z*, in all kinds of clever, funny ways. So, the closed fist for *A* knocked at a door; the four raised fingers for *B* moved to show the door opening, the cupped shape for *C* searched around to find something. Boogie could never have come up with something that creative in a million billion years.

For the final number on the program, all the kids in the Deaf after-school program sang along to "America the Beautiful" in ASL. It was easier for Boogie to pick out some of the signs this time because he already knew the words.

At the end of the program, the Longwood campers started whistling and cheering before Peg and Sally signaled to them to clap in the finger-waving Deaf way. Boogie saw that even James was clapping. He *should* be clapping. James couldn't dance like that *or* tell stories like that *or* sign along to a song.

Then it was time for refreshments and trying to sign with the Deaf kids. Boogie wished he knew the signs for *amazing* and *fabulous* and *awesome*. But he didn't.

Were they just supposed to go up to

somebody and start asking one of the questions they had learned? Boogie could tell the others felt shy, too, because Nixie, Nolan, and Vera hung back with him. Nixie didn't look eager to ask if anybody had a dog with newborn puppies. Nolan didn't look ready to demonstrate all the signs he had mastered. Vera looked as if she wanted to flee to a corner of the room and curl up with her art notebook. The other Longwood campers were standing fixed in place, too.

Somebody had to do something.

"Let's go up to the dancer kids," Boogie made himself say. "Come on." He led the way to the food table.

Hi, Boogie signed. He pointed to himself and finger-spelled his name. Nolan and Nixie followed his example, but Vera stood frozen, her face looking like the expression for signing *scared*.

The four dancers finger-spelled their names. Luckily, Nolan recognized all the letters they signed and said each name aloud: Ben (Boogie had recognized the *B* and *E*, at least), Sam, Amy, and Lily.

Now what?

Boogie jumped in first again. He pointed to himself for *I*, crossed his arms in front of his chest for *love*, pointed to the dancers, and then made up his own sign for *dance*, by doing a crazy little jig.

The other kids laughed, but not in a mean James kind of way. The girl named Amy showed Boogie the real sign for *dance*, made with two fingers of one hand twirling upside down over the other hand, like two dancing legs on a dance floor.

Nixie jumped into the conversation next. She signed, as Boogie had known she would, *I want a dog*.

Two of the dancers pointed to themselves and made the sign *I have a dog*; one pointed to herself and made the sign for *I have a cat*. The fourth one made a sign with one hand wrapped over the other hand, formed into a fist with the thumb poking out, and suddenly Boogie guessed it.

"Turtle!" he shouted, forgetting for a moment that the Deaf kids couldn't hear him. But the turtle-owning kid must have understood somehow, because he gave a big grin of approval.

Nolan asked one of the questions from Peg and Sally's list: *What is your favorite food?*

Boogie hoped the answers would be foods from the Deaf family's breakfast and lunch videos. But when one kid held his hand to his mouth and moved it back and forth as if he was licking it, Boogie instantly guessed that one, too. Ice cream! He felt another thrill of understanding.

Nixie kept firing off questions: *Do you like eggs? Do you like milk? Do you like toast? Do you like orange juice?* Sometimes the other kids would correct one of her signs, in a friendly way, and Nixie would whack the side of her head, clearly her made-up sign for *Oops! I got it wrong!*

Before long, everyone was laughing, even Vera, although she hadn't yet signed a single word.

Too soon it was time to board the bus to return to Longwood.

Peg and Sally made a farewell announcement, Peg speaking while Sally signed. "Thank you so much for sharing such a wonderful program with us today! Now we want to invite you to come for a program at our school, two weeks from today, on the last day of our sign-language camp to show all we have learned."

The kids from Laurent Clerc School twisted their fingers in the air as a Deaf camp teacher signed a response, which Peg translated: *We would love to come!*

Boogie gulped.

What on earth could they do that would be anywhere near as good as the program today?

He already knew the answer: nothing.

They could sign the alphabet to the tune of the ABC song.

Period.

And even with his new practicing, Boogie wasn't sure he could do that.

★ seven ★

It snowed again Friday night. On Saturday morning, the sun shone on a glistening world of white. It was perfect weather for outdoor luge, or at least for outdoor sledding.

It was also the perfect chance to earn money to buy a sad little Bing a brand-new Doggie-Dog.

As his brothers watched cartoons in the family room, Boogie bundled up and slipped into the garage to find the snow shovel.

He started by shoveling the path from the front door to the sidewalk. Then he kept on going and shoveled the heavy wet snow on the two long sidewalks along the edges of their corner lot.

The *very* heavy and *very* wet snow on the *very* long sidewalks.

And there was still was the *very* long and *very* wide driveway.

Boogie's parents didn't pay him for doing chores, like loading the dishwasher or carrying out the trash. One time when Boogie had suggested payment, his mother had asked him if he was going to pay *her* for cooking the meals, cleaning the house, and making sure four boys didn't destroy it.

This was different, though. Snow shoveling wasn't a *chore*. It was *work*. Some grown-ups had snow-shoveling businesses, showing up with trucks filled with snow blowers to clear dozens of driveways for tons of money. Shoveling one driveway was enough for Boogie. And he didn't need tons of money. He only needed eighteen dollars plus four dollars for shipping. Well, minus the sixty-seven cents he already had, but that was hardly worth counting.

When he came inside, his brothers were still lying on the floor staring at the TV. His father was off at work, of course. Bitter cold weather meant freezing pipes, which meant bursting pipes, which meant water everywhere, which meant: *Call the plumber!*

He found his mother in the kitchen frying bacon and scrambling eggs.

"*You,*" she said, sweeping Boogie into a hug, "are my *hero!*"

Boogie felt himself beaming.

"When I heard someone shoveling the driveway, I thought it must be some kind neighbor coming to our rescue, knowing your dad was off at work and I was busy watching little boys. But it wasn't a neighbor; it was my very own superhero son!"

Boogie felt his grin growing even bigger and wider.

"And you know what I appreciated most?" his mother asked.

Boogie shook his head.

"I didn't have to *ask* you to do it. I didn't have to *pay* you to do it. You just went out there and did it out of the goodness of your heart."

But . . . but . . .

Couldn't you shovel snow out of the goodness of your heart and still get paid eighteen dollars plus four dollars for shipping?

Apparently not.

Maybe he could go ask the neighbors if they'd pay him actual money for shoveling. But his arms ached, and his shoulders ached, and his back ached; he ached all over. He hadn't known how exhausting the goodness of your heart could be.

It still felt good to hear his mother's praise.

But praise plus money to buy a new Doggie-Dog would have been even better.

Nolan came over that afternoon to join in sledding with Boogie and his brothers on the hill at the park near their house. Luckily, all the burst pipes had gotten fixed that morning, so Boogie's dad was there, too.

Outdoor sledding in the snow was a lot more fun than indoor sledding on the stairs. And if any sled crashed into anything, this time his dad would get the blame, not Boogie. Plus, it was so great to have his dad at home. If only his dad didn't have to work such long hours.

As Boogie and his dad dragged the sleds

back up the hill, a brilliant idea popped into Boogie's head for earning money *and* helping his dad have more time for family fun.

"Dad?" he asked. "What if you had an assistant? Someone to go with you and help you fix the pipes and unclog the toilets?"

Should he add that this would be an assistant who got paid money to help, not an assistant who helped out of the goodness of his heart?

"Plumbing is pretty much a one-person job," his dad said. "We work in some small and cramped spaces."

"*I* could fit in a small and cramped space," Boogie said. "*I* could be your assistant."

"You?" His father gave a bark of laughter, but then sighed. "Son, there'll be plenty of time for you to do work like that when you're grown up. Now is your time just to be a kid."

Boogie sighed, too.

If he could unclog *one* toilet, and earn enough money to buy *one* new Doggie-Dog, then he could go back to just being a kid. But he could tell his father had already given his answer.

Back at the house afterward, in a combination of words and signs, Boogie told Nolan, "I shoveled snow to make money to buy a new dog." Instead of saying *shovel*, he made a shoveling motion; instead of saying *snow*, he fluttered his fingers in the air; instead of saying *money*, he tapped his circled fingers onto his hand as if placing coins there. He made the sign for *dog* twice, hoping Nolan would know that meant Doggie-Dog. He didn't want to say the words aloud, or else his parents and brothers, who were in the family room with them, would hear.

"But it didn't work out," he finished. Nolan made the *sad* sign. "So now I don't know what to do."

Nolan pointed to himself, made the sign for *money*, and then held his hands toward Boogie in the sign for *give*.

Boogie signed *no* and then added the sign for *thank you*, so Nolan's feelings wouldn't be hurt. This was something he needed to do by himself, even if had no idea how he was going to do it.

"What are you guys talking about?" T.J. demanded. "Is that a secret code?

It was, sort of. Boogie and Nolan grinned at each other.

Bing had been watching the whole time, his thumb jammed into his mouth. He had been sucking his thumb more since he lost Doggie-Dog, too, and talking even less.

Hadn't Peg said something on the first day of class about teaching ASL signs to very little kids to help them show their feelings even if they weren't good at speaking words yet?

Boogie picked Bing up and set him on his lap, so they faced each other.

"Here," Boogie said. "*Happy.*" He made the sign to go with it. Bing took his thumb out of his mouth and used his hands to copy Boogie.

"*Sad,*" Boogie said, and signed. Bing copied that one, too.

When Boogie signed, "*Scared,*" Bing burst out laughing, and Boogie laughed, too.

But if only Bing could be giggling while cuddling a soft new Doggie-Dog.

★ ★ ★

On Monday, Peg and Sally skipped the usual ABCs drill—hooray, hooray!—and started right in on talking about the camp's final program, the Signing Showcase.

"Your families and friends are invited, and as you know, our new friends from Laurent Clerc School have already told us they're coming, too. Colleen got permission for us to hold it in the auditorium. So as we continue to learn new signs every day during this week and next, we'll also be preparing for our wonderful program."

Boogie tried to imagine what their wonderful program could possibly be.

"We'll start off the showcase with our ABC song," Peg said.

Great.

Peg went on, "We'll do the song a few times to help our friends and families learn some of the letters to sign along with us."

That sounded a little bit better. At least it would use up more time.

"We'll sign the words to some simple songs," Peg and Sally went on. "If we have time to prepare, we may add a short skit or two. We'll finish up with a Parade of Animals, where we'll show our audience some of the most fun animal signs."

It didn't sound so bad, really. Boogie had been afraid he'd have to go up onstage and do something all by himself. He wasn't shy the way Vera was, but between his ABC mess-ups and James's constant teasing, it was hard to feel like standing up in front of a whole audience of people and having them laugh at him, too. But he wouldn't mind being in an animal parade along with everyone else.

He tuned back in to Peg talking. "For the whole program we will have a master of ceremonies, or an emcee, who will greet our guests and introduce the acts. This Friday you will get to vote on who that will be."

Boogie saw lots of kids looking over at Nolan. Of the sixteen campers, every single one would vote for Nolan, except for Nolan, who would be too modest to vote for himself. Well, maybe James wouldn't even bother to vote.

At least the Signing Showcase emcee would be terrific. Boogie just hoped the rest of them could do a good enough job that the Deaf kids would like their program as much as he and his friends had liked theirs.

★ eight ★

On Tuesday they began practicing the Parade of the Animals for the Signing Showcase.

Boogie was assigned the best animal by far, in his opinion: the penguin. He got to hold his hands stiffly at his sides and waddle from side to side. But all the animal signs were terrific. Nolan's elephant moved his hand forward from his nose like an elephant trunk, his arm swaying at the end. Vera's timid little mouse touched her nose a few times. Nixie was given the dog sign, of course. Peg and Sally knew better than to give that sign to anyone else.

After the first run-through of the animal parade, James caught Boogie's eye. With a smirk, he imitated Boogie's penguin to make it look as ridiculous as possible. James had the second-best animal: the chest-thumping gorilla. But James made sure to look like a bored gorilla, rolling his eyes as he did a few half-hearted thumps, so everyone would know he still thought the whole thing was dumb.

But maybe Boogie *had* looked foolish making the penguin sign. On the second time through the program, he saw even Nixie and Vera whispering to each other behind their hands as he trundled by. Some other kids were actually laughing. Were they giggling because penguins are funny to look at? Or were they making fun of *him*, Boogie?

Wednesday they worked in small groups learning the signs to go along with the words in simple songs like "Twinkle, Twinkle, Little Star" and "Five Little Monkeys Jumping on the Bed." They weren't trying to sign every word, just *twinkle* (Peg said it was really the sign for *sparkle*), *little*, *star*, and *wonder*.

Vera made her usual frown of concentration as she signed *five*, *monkeys*, *jumping*, and *bed*. The song was supposed to be funny, but you'd never guess it from looking at Vera's face.

As each monkey fell off the bed, she looked as anxious as if real monkeys were having constant head injuries.

Nixie pointed this out in her usual blunt way.

"The monkeys are fine, Vera!" she said with a giggle. "No real monkeys were harmed in the making of this song!"

"I hate when people look at me," Vera said in a low voice. "And I hate it even more if they look at me while I'm making mistakes."

"You never make any mistakes!" Nixie told her. "I'm the one who makes mistakes!"

Boogie had wondered if she was going to say, *Boogie's the one who makes mistakes*. But it was easy to remember the signs for words like *monkey* (scratching your sides), *jumping* (making two fingers jump off the palm of the other hand), and *bed* (laying your head on the side of your folded hands, as if they were a pillow). Plus, living in his house was like being in a real-life song about four little monkeys jumping everywhere.

"Anyway," Nixie added, "people look at you when you play the piano in recitals."

Vera wasn't only the best artist Boogie knew; she also took piano lessons.

"I hate that, too," Vera said. "Not the piano part, but the recital part. At the Signing Showcase, I'm going to hate the people-looking-at-me part *and* the talking-to-people-I-don't-know part. When we went to visit the Deaf school, I didn't sign a single thing to anybody. If I don't sign a single thing this time, they'll think I'm the most unfriendly person in the world."

"You'll do fine," Nolan tried to reassure her. "We'll all do fine."

Boogie could tell Vera thought even Nolan was wrong about some things some of the time.

Later that afternoon, when Boogie went to get a snack during the camp break, he heard his name when some kids were talking by the food table.

"The thing about Boogie—" one girl was saying. She broke off when she saw Boogie approaching. So Boogie didn't know how she had planned to finish the sentence.

What was the thing about Boogie?

The thing about Boogie is he thinks he's so funny, but he really isn't.

The thing about Boogie is he keeps messing up all the time.

The thing about Boogie is he's so much worse at everything than Nolan is.

Sometimes when Boogie got a snack, he tried to balance a cube of cheese on the end of his nose or make false teeth out of an orange rind.

This time he decided he wasn't hungry after all.

★ ★ ★

Nolan was acting strange in camp on Thursday. Maybe not strange, exactly, but Boogie caught Nolan staring at him and then looking away suddenly when Boogie turned in his direction. Maybe Nolan was nervous about the camp vote for the Signing Showcase emcee. There was no way he wouldn't win, but Boogie had overheard James say *Showoff* the other day when Nolan already knew the sign for *star* even though the rest of the camp hadn't learned it yet.

If Boogie was truly Nolan's best friend, he'd be—what did they call it?—Nolan's *campaign manager*. He'd make sure everyone was going to vote for the best signer *and* the best friend ever.

During the break Boogie wandered over to some kids who were sitting in the back of the room.

"You're voting for Nolan tomorrow, aren't you?" Boogie blurted out.

Two of the girls exchanged glances.

"Maybe," one of them said.

"Maybe not," the other one said.

How could anyone not vote for Nolan?

Boogie heard the other kids smothering giggles as he walked away.

When camp was over, as Boogie and Nolan sat waiting for their parents, Nolan suddenly pulled a lumpy bundle from his backpack.

He thrust it toward Boogie. "Open it."

What could it be?

It wasn't Boogie's birthday.

There was no reason Nolan would be giving him a present.

The package felt squishy, almost like a stuffed animal about the size and shape of Doggie-Dog.

But Nolan had already offered to buy Bing's Doggie-Dog, and Boogie had already told him no.

Nolan wasn't Bing's big brother.

Boogie was.

Nolan wasn't the one who was supposed to get Bing a new Doggie-Dog.

Boogie was.

Boogie pulled at the tape on the package. Inside, he could see white fur with black spots.

Doggie-Dog had white fur with black spots.

As Boogie froze, Nolan reached over and pulled the brand-new Doggie-Dog from its padded envelope.

Boogie swallowed hard.

"Now Bing can have it right away," Nolan said, his voice suddenly sounding less confident than usual. "It's not your fault you didn't get paid for shoveling the snow."

But it *was* Boogie's fault he never saved any of his money while Nolan saved all of his.

"*You're* the one who really bought it," Nolan went on. "It was *your* idea. I just helped a tiny bit with the money part."

Like paying the entire eighteen dollars, plus

four dollars for shipping. Maybe even more, so the package would come extra-fast.

Boogie tried to force a smile. But he could tell it wasn't a very good smile.

"What?" Nolan said. "I just thought . . . I knew how much you wanted Bing to have it. I just wanted to help."

"You always help!" Boogie burst out. "You help everybody with everything all the time! *I'm* the reason Doggie-Dog got ruined, and *you're* the reason Bing got a new one. *You* do everything right, and *I* do everything wrong!"

"That's not true," Nolan said. "I didn't do *this* right. And you do *lots* of things right."

"Like what?" Boogie demanded. "Name one thing I've ever done right."

But before Nolan could answer, there was Boogie's mother coming toward them, with T.J., Gib, and Bing trailing behind her. Quickly Boogie shoved the new Doggie-Dog back into its package.

"Ready?" Boogie's mother asked.

Without another word to Nolan, Boogie followed her, so he didn't have to watch Nolan struggling to answer his question.

★ ★ ★

"Look what Nolan got for you!" Boogie said to Bing that evening when he and Bing were finally alone in the family room.

T.J. and Gib were both having a time-out for trying to turn Bear into a polar bear by emptying a canister of flour all over him. Their mother was busy brushing off Bear, as well as vacuuming up the flour that lay thick like new-fallen snow on the kitchen floor.

From behind his back Boogie produced the brand-new Doggie-Dog.

Bing stared at it, his face squinched up in puzzlement. Boogie had to admit the new Doggie-Dog looked and felt very different from the old Doggie-Dog. One was bright white with black spots; the other had become dirty gray with faded spots. One was firm and solid; the other had been soft and limp.

"It's Doggie-Dog!" Boogie said.

His little brother didn't reach out to cuddle it, so Boogie waggled the new dog and made it talk in a high, squeaky voice. "I'm your new Doggie-Dog! I'm here to be your friend!"

Bing looked up at Boogie and made the

sign Boogie had taught him for *sad*. But Boogie didn't even need the sign; he could see real tears starting to trickle down Bing's cheeks.

Over the last few days Boogie had taught Bing some other signs, too. Now Bing made the tap-and-snap sign for *dog* and pointed emphatically to himself, and then made the sign for *dog* a second time and pointed to himself again.

Bing didn't want *this* Doggie-Dog. He wanted *his* Doggie-Dog.

Wonderful.

Maybe Bing *had* already started to forget about Doggie-Dog. Maybe Boogie's mom had been right, after all, when she said that stuffed animals were more trouble than they were worth.

This was your *idea*, Nolan had told him, trying to make Boogie feel better.

Now Boogie felt even worse.

★ nine ★

Friday's camp was so busy with practice for the Signing Showcase that a full hour passed before Colleen whispered something to Peg, and then Sally switched the lights off and on to get everyone's attention.

"We almost forgot the most important thing we have to do today," Peg said, while Sally signed.

Boogie loved watching Sally's busy hands as he tried to figure out exactly which sign meant *forgot* and which sign meant *important*.

If only he was better at sign language.

If only he was better at being a brother, too.

If only he was better at everything.

"We have to vote for our showcase emcee," Peg and Sally continued. "We teachers could have picked someone ourselves, but this is *your* camp, *your* showcase, *your* chance to shine, so everyone gets to do the choosing here, campers *and* teachers, all of us."

Colleen passed out a pencil and a small square of paper to each camper. Boogie was glad it was the kind of vote where people didn't have to raise their hands in front of everyone. He didn't want to be mad at anyone who didn't vote for Nolan.

Boogie covered his paper with his hand as he wrote *Nolan*, even though he knew everyone would be writing the same thing.

Colleen collected the ballots. It took only a minute for Peg and Sally to count them.

"We have a winner," Peg said with a smile. "In fact, it was almost unanimous. The emcee for our show will be . . ."

Nolan Nanda!

"Boogie Bass," Peg finished.

Was this a joke? A joke that was James's idea, so the worst signer in the camp would stand up onstage in front of everyone looking completely ridiculous?

But everyone was clapping, including

Nolan, Nixie, and Vera, and they wouldn't be cheering for him if this was a prank. Peg and Sally were clapping in the Deaf finger-twirling way.

"Boogie," Peg said, "this means you'll have to do a lot of work this coming week to learn your lines. Are you ready to show how hard you can work?"

Boogie was too stunned to do anything but nod.

"All right, campers, time for a break!"

It was all wrong.

It was totally unfair.

Nolan was ten thousand times better at signing than anybody in the room except for Peg and Sally.

"I'm sorry," Boogie choked out, finally finding his voice. "Nolan, you're the one who deserves this, not me. *I* voted for you. I told other kids to vote for you, too."

"Are you crazy?" Nixie demanded. "Nolan *wanted* you to be it. He wanted you to be it even more than you wanted him to be it! If you ever run for president of the United States, Nolan will get millions of people to vote for you!"

Boogie suddenly understood.

The others had voted for him because Nolan told them to, so Boogie would stop feeling so bad about himself.

"Oh," Boogie said in a small voice. "I get it now."

For one teensy-weensy moment he had almost let himself think maybe he had miraculously become a good signer.

"Nolan talked to everybody, but it was actually Vera's idea for you to be the emcee," Nixie said.

Vera's idea?

"Remember when we went to Laurent Clerc School?" Vera asked. "You were the one who went up to the Deaf dancers and started signing, and then all of sudden everyone was talking to everyone else, and it wasn't weird and awkward anymore. *You* were the one who made everyone feel happy and welcome, and that's what the emcee is supposed to do, right?"

"And remember how you were the best at doing the feelings signs?" Nixie asked.

"Peg and Sally even made you show how well you did them to the whole camp."

"And when James made fun of you, you just laughed it off, because you're so nice to everybody," Nolan added. "Guess what? *James* voted for you, too. When I told him we thought you should be the emcee, he looked embarrassed and said he didn't know why he keeps on teasing you."

They all sounded like they meant it.

"But I still get *M* and *N* mixed up in the ABCs," Boogie protested. "I still might trip on the stage and fall flat on my face."

Nolan, Nixie, and Vera gave the same shrug, as if to say, *So?*

Maybe the point of learning a new language wasn't to be perfect about every word and every letter. Maybe the point was to share what you thought and felt so other people would understand, and to be able to understand them when they shared their thoughts and feelings with you.

"Everyone voted for you," Nixie said.

"Even the teachers," Vera said.

"*You're* the only one who didn't vote for you," Nolan said.

All Boogie could do was make the sign for *wow*, waving his spread-out hand sideways near his chest, over and over again.

At home that night Boogie found the new Doggie-Dog lying ignored on the floor by Bing's bed. If the door to Bing's room hadn't been shut, Bear would have chewed up a second Doggie-Dog head. But this one was probably too new to taste very good. It didn't have Bing's smell all over it, Bing's *love* all over it, the way the old Doggie-Dog had.

Boogie went to get the headless body of the old Doggie-Dog out of the bottom of his bureau drawer.

It looked as sad as you'd expect an old worn-out stuffed toy without a head to look. But this was still the *real* Doggie-Dog, the Doggie-Dog Bing loved. The Doggie-Dog Bing *needed*.

Boogie had another idea.

This might be a terrible idea, but maybe it wasn't.

If the whole sign-language camp had voted for him to be emcee for the Signing Showcase, he might be able to do *something* right.

But if this idea turned out to be terrible, it was going to be very terrible.

Boogie found his mother's sewing box on the top shelf in her closet. One time, T.J. and Gib had taken her special sewing scissors and used them to cut open the beanbag chair in the family room because they wanted to see if the beans inside were the kind people could eat. Ever since then there was a rule against any boy touching the sewing box for any reason whatsoever.

Boogie took the box and carried it back to his bedroom.

"Bing!" he called.

Please let this work. Please let this work.

As soon as Bing came into the room and saw the old headless Doggie-Dog, he grabbed it and hugged it as if he would never let it go.

"Watch this," Boogie said, as if he was about to perform a magic trick.

With his mother's extra-sharp sewing scissors, he carefully snipped the threads of the seam on the back of the new Doggie-Dog and scooped out the stuffing. Bits of fluff fell onto the floor like the flour from T.J. and Gib's polar bear project.

As Bing watched, wide-eyed, Boogie gently pried the old Doggie-Dog away from his hands. Without its head, the old Doggie-Dog was smaller now. Plus, its stuffing had lost a lot of its stuffiness. So the old Doggie-Dog fit inside the empty body of the new Doggie-Dog. Grown-ups were always saying that the most important thing about you wasn't what you looked like on the outside, but who you were on the inside. Boogie hoped Bing would agree.

He found a needle, already threaded, stuck into his mom's pincushion, and did his best to sew up the open seam at the back. Maybe the next Longwood Elementary After-School Superstars program would be a sewing camp so big brothers could learn how to do a perfect job stitching up their little brothers' stuffed animals. But when he was done, he thought it looked good enough.

"What do you think, Bing?" he asked, holding out the new-and-old Doggie-Dog to him.

Would Bing start crying again? Would he push this Doggie-Dog away, too?

A slow smile spread across Bing's face. "*My* Doggie-Dog!" Bing said, cradling it close to his chest. "*My* Doggie-Dog!"

Boogie felt a huge smile spreading across his own face.

He made the sign for *happy* to Bing.

And Bing made it back to Boogie.

★ ten ★

Boogie stood straight and tall in a black suit that was a size too small, a hand-me-down from an older cousin. His mop of curls was as neatly combed as a mop of curls could be. After practicing for the whole week one-on-one with Sally, and at home with Bing and Doggie-Dog, he was ready. Or as ready as he would ever be.

The Longwood auditorium wasn't a real auditorium. It was just a semicircular space in the middle of the school, where the audience sat on low carpeted risers, while the performers stood on a small raised platform in front that served as the stage. For the Signing Showcase the space was packed. From his spot at the side of the stage, Boogie could see the Laurent Clerc kids talking away with their hands. He hoped they wouldn't think it was pathetic to watch kids who were the same age as them but who were just now learning their ABCs. But everyone had to start somewhere.

Lots of parents, siblings, and friends were there. He saw Nolan's mom and dad and his two older sisters. Would they think Nolan should have been the emcee, not him? But they were as kind as Nolan. Vera's mom was there in a purple business suit, looking fancier than most of the other parents. Nixie's dad and mom had both taken time off from work to come. Boogie hoped that one of these days Nixie would be able to wear them down and finally get a dog of her own. A girl named Lucy, who had been at coding camp with them last month, was there with her big sister.

But all these people together didn't make as much noise as T.J. and Gib, who were running up and down the risers as if riser racing was an Olympic event and they were sprinting toward a medal.

"T.J.! Gib!" he heard his mother saying. "Boys, I'm not going to tell you this again. Boys!"

Only Bing sat quietly, clutching Doggie-Dog. When his mom had tucked Bing into bed a week ago, Boogie had lingered at the door to see if she noticed the return of Doggie-Dog. At first she had given Doggie-Dog a kiss the same way she had always done after first kissing Bing. Then she did a double take.

"Where did *this* come from?" she asked Boogie.

Thank goodness Boogie had remembered to return her sewing box to the closet! He could feel his proud grin giving him away.

"But I thought we had agreed not to keep on bothering with this," she said.

Then, at the sight of Bing and Doggie-Dog cuddled together, her face had softened.

"Where did you *get* it?" she asked Boogie.

Should he have told her Nolan had gotten it for him? But he was the one who had turned the new Doggie-Dog into a Doggie-Dog Bing would still love the same old way. So all he had said was, "Nolan and I got it together," which was totally the truth.

Now Peg switched the lights off and on.

The room fell silent. Even T.J. and Gib plopped down in place. It was time for the showcase to begin.

Boogie walked to the microphone. He was going to speak into it for the people in the audience who didn't know sign language, which was just about everybody except for the kids from Laurent Clerc. As he spoke, he'd sign.

"Good afternoon!" he said and signed, smiling his biggest smile because it *was* a good afternoon. It was a *great* afternoon! "My name is Boogie Bass. Welcome to our program! We are going to show you all we have learned!"

He spoke and signed slowly. The Deaf kids, the real signers, would have moved their hands so much faster. But he knew he was doing a good job.

When he introduced the ABC song, he invited the audience to sign along. Would the Deaf kids do it, or would they think it was too babyish? But they did, and in fact, they ended up showing people in the audience how to hold their fingers in the correct positions. If only they had been at camp when Boogie and his friends had been learning! By the time the song had been sung half a dozen times, lots of people were laughing at how much fun it had been to sing the alphabet in this completely new way.

The other songs went well, too. Boogie saw that James was *not* rolling his eyes and giving his usual sullen scowl. His fingers twirling for "Twinkle, Twinkle, Little Star" were twinkling as happily as everybody else's.

Over the last few days Sally and Peg had added a couple of short skits to the program, including a signing solo for Nolan. For his act, he did math problems by using number signs, his fingers moving almost as fast as if he was Deaf himself. Boogie didn't know if the emcee was supposed to clap, but when Nolan took his bow, Boogie couldn't help proudly twisting his hands high in the air. It was perfect that one best friend was the emcee and the other one had a special part in the program, too.

The program ended with the Parade of Animals. Even though Boogie, as emcee, hadn't taken part in any of the other demonstrations, he joined in this one. Since real-life penguins looked as if they were wearing black suits

with shiny white shirts, Boogie felt especially penguin-like dressed up in his emcee outfit. The audience laughed for him appreciatively. He did stumble over his untied shoelace as he left the stage, but Nolan, Nixie, and Vera had been right: it didn't matter.

Once the program was over, it was time for refreshments. Boogie led the way to the group of Deaf kids, with his friends following. After a moment of hesitation, James came with them.

Great job! one kid signed, not just for Boogie, but for all of them.

Another kid, with a puzzled look on his face, finger-spelled Boogie's name. Then the kid moved his fingers down from his nose in a way that had to be the sign for *booger*.

James cracked up totally, and then the Deaf kid cracked up, too. It was impossible for Boogie to keep from laughing along with them.

When he was finally able to stop laughing, he tried to explain.

No, he signed. He spelled his name again, and he did the sign the Deaf kids had taught him last time for *dance*. Then he boogied in place, and before he knew it, all the kids, Deaf and hearing, were laughing harder than ever.

After that, everyone was talking and signing like old friends. James signed that he liked to play basketball, holding his hands up as if he was making a basket. Finally even Vera signed that she liked art, drawing a zigzag line with her pinkie finger across the palm of her other hand.

The dancer girl they had met last time, Amy, had a notebook with her. She opened it to a blank page and held it out to Vera, along with a pencil.

Flushing, Vera shook her head.

"Vera!" Nixie said. "Come on, draw something!"

"I can't," Vera whispered frantically.

"You totally can!" Nixie replied.

Shyly, Vera took the notebook and pencil and sat down in a corner of the room. Five minutes later she returned and handed the notebook to Amy. Boogie could see Vera had drawn a girl who looked exactly like Amy, with two pigtails, a freckled nose, and a short twirly skirt.

Amy signed *wow*.

Drawing was a kind of language, too.

Boogie felt someone tugging on his legs.

It was Bing, still holding on to Doggie-Dog, with his mother close behind. T.J. and Gib were back at their Olympic riser race. It was clear his mother had given up trying to make them stop. At least Bear wasn't there to be barking at their heels as they ran.

"You were wonderful!" Boogie's mother said, crushing him into a hug. "I took a video on my phone to show your dad."

When she let him go, she took his face in her hands and looked into his eyes.

"I have to admit I was surprised when you told us you were picked to be the emcee. I guess I just thought . . ."

She let the sentence trail off, but Boogie finished it for her.

"You thought it would be Nolan. Because Nolan is better at everything than I am, right? *He* wouldn't forget to close a door so Bear wouldn't chew Doggie-Dog. *He* wouldn't break your favorite vase doing indoor luge."

His voice came out more wobbly than he wanted it to.

"Oh, Boogie," his mother said.

Now her voice was the one that sounded wobbly.

"Oh, honey, people say things they don't really mean all the time when they're upset. Boogie, look at me. Who's the big brother who can get Bing to smile and laugh when nobody else can? Who's the big brother who knew how much Bing needed a new Doggie-Dog and somehow made that happen? When even his own mother didn't? Who's the kid I'm so very proud of today?"

"Me?" Boogie asked.

"*You*," his mother said.

Bing was sitting on the floor now, with Doggie-Dog facing him. He pointed to himself, crossed both hands across his heart, and pointed at Doggie-Dog.

"Who taught him to do that?" Boogie's mother asked. "Never mind, I know the answer to *that* one."

Copying Bing, she signed to Boogie, as Bing had signed to Doggie-Dog: *I love you.*

Boogie didn't need to sign anything in reply. He could feel his great big smile saying everything.

Some Facts about Sign Language

There are approximately seventy million Deaf people worldwide and (by some estimates) three hundred different sign languages.

Sign language differs from country to country, even when two countries speak the same language. In fact, American Sign Language has more in common with French Sign Language than it does with British Sign Language, because it was developed with the assistance of Frenchman Laurent Clerc.

In American Sign Language, the alphabet is signed using just one hand. But in some other sign languages, such as British Sign Language, two hands are used. Most sign languages use less finger-spelling than ASL, and some don't use finger-spelling at all.

When you are asking a question in ASL related to who, where, what, why, and when, keep your eyebrows down. When you are asking a yes/no question, or a rhetorical question (a question where you don't really expect an answer), keep your eyebrows up.

The signs of American Sign Language don't stand for English *words*, but for their *meanings*. So the English word *right* has two meanings: one is the opposite of *wrong*, the other is the opposite of *left*. These have two different signs in ASL, just as they do in many languages other than English.

When you are talking to a Deaf person, speak directly to them, looking them in the eye, even if an interpreter is there. It is rude to look at the interpreter while speaking, as if the Deaf person wasn't there.

Dogs that cannot hear (as well as dogs with Deaf owners) can learn to obey simple sign-language commands just as hearing dogs can obey simple spoken commands.

In a study to see if gorillas can communicate using human language, even though their vocal cords cannot form spoken words, Koko the gorilla learned more than a thousand signs of what her caregiver, Francine Patterson, called Gorilla Sign Language. But Koko was never able to learn the complex grammar of any sign language (the rules for how words should be put together in sentences). Only human beings can do that.

If you want to learn more about sign language, especially how to make particular signs, there are many resources online where you can see exactly how to do this. Make sure you find videos by credentialed ASL teachers, particularly members of the Deaf community. One good one is the American Sign Language University website at lifeprint.com.

Acknowledgments

My beloved editor, Margaret Ferguson, has an uncanny gift for figuring out what each book needs to help it be the best and truest version of itself. Then, just when I think I have the book in its final, flawless form, Chandra Wohleber offers insightful corrections I would cringe to have missed. Brilliant illustrator Grace Zong knows my characters even better than I do and makes them look exactly as I imagined them, only more so. Kerry Martin created an adorable design for the entire After-School Superstars series that makes me pick up each title with a tingle of happiness.

My superstar agent, Stephen Fraser, cheers me on just as supportively as Nolan, Nixie, and Vera encourage Boogie. Writer friends offered critiques on crucial drafts: heartfelt thanks to the Writing Roosters (Jennifer Bertman, Jennifer Sims, Laura Perdew, Vanessa Appleby, and especially Tracy Abell) and to Leslie O'Kane.

I give special thanks to Kayla O'Connor for helping me research sign-language camps for hearing kids and come up with some of the activities featured in the story. St. Bernadette Catholic Parish in Lakewood, Colorado, allowed me to sit in on several sessions of their Beginning American Sign Language Video Course, taught by instructor Sue Metz and teaching assistant Tom Metz, with interpreter Jeanie Mamula. It was a gift to be taught by these two Deaf instructors. The course made use of the ASL video *Meet the Bravo Family*, which inspired the videos Boogie watches in his camp.

Finally, Renate Rose from Gallaudet University read the entire draft of the manuscript and offered fabulously helpful suggestions to make sure that ASL and Deaf culture were presented accurately and with respect. I am beyond grateful to her for this assistance.

Claudia Mills is the acclaimed author of more than sixty books for children, including the Franklin School Friends series and the middle-grade novel *Zero Tolerance*. She recently received the Kerlan Award. She lives in Boulder, Colorado.

Grace Zong has illustrated many books for children, including *Goldy Luck and the Three Pandas* by Natasha Yim and *Mrs. McBee Leaves Room 3* by Gretchen Brandenburg McLellan. She divides her time between South Korea and New York.